GREAT WRITERS

OSCAR WILDE

CRESCENT BOOKS
NEW YORK • AVENEL

This edition published 1995 by Crescent Books,
distributed by Random House Value Publishing, Inc.
40 Engelhard Avenue, Avenel, New Jersey 07001.

Random House
New York • Toronto • London • Sydney • Auckland

First published 1994 by Aurum Press Ltd,
25 Bedford Avenue, London WC1B 3AT

A CIP catalog record for this book is available from the Library of Congress.

ISBN 0-517-14254-6

Printed and bound in China by Regent Publishing Services

10 9 8 7 6 5 4 3 2 1

All quotations are by Oscar Wilde, unless otherwise stated.

I was a man who stood in symbolic relations to the art and culture of my age...The gods had given me almost everything. I had genius, a distinguished name, high social position, brilliancy, intellectual daring; I made art a philosophy, and philosophy an art: I altered the minds of men and the colour of things: there was nothing I said or did that did not make people wonder...I treated Art as the supreme reality, and life as a mere mode of fiction: I awoke the imagination of my century so that it created myth and legend around me: I summed up all systems in a phrase, and all existence in an epigram.

DE PROFUNDIS

'GRAND, MISTY, AND OSSIANIC'

I am not English, I am Irish – which is quite another thing.

A Joan of Arc was never meant for marriage, and so here I am…rocking a cradle in which lies my second son – a babe of one month old the 16th of this month and as large and fine and handsome and healthy as if he were three months. He is to be called Oscar Fingal Wilde. Is not that grand, misty, and Ossianic?

LADY WILDE, OSCAR'S MOTHER

We Irish are too poetical to be poets; we are a nation of brilliant failures, but we are the greatest talkers since the Greeks.

He was unpopular with his schoolmates, as a large, ungainly boy with inert habits and an unfortunate fluency in devising apt but acid nicknames is certain to be. His own, which annoyed him, was Grey Crow…untidy, inclined to flop about, slovenly in both appearance and dress, with hands and face always in need of washing and with nails showing signs of mourning, he made no deep impression on his fellows, and such impression as he did make was generally unfavourable…Any forecast of distinction that might have been made about him then would probably have been derided. His mother's assertion that he was 'a wonderful boy' was, no doubt, regarded as the nonsense of a fond mamma.

ST JOHN ERVINE ABOUT WILDE AT PORTORA ROYAL SCHOOL, ENNISKILLEN

It must not be forgotten that though by culture Wilde was a citizen of all civilised capitals, he was at root a very Irish Irishman, and as such, a foreigner everywhere but in Ireland.

GEORGE BERNARD SHAW

The two great turning points of my life were when my father sent me to Oxford, and when society sent me to prison.

DE PROFUNDIS

I'll be a poet, a writer, a dramatist. Somehow or other I'll be famous, and if not famous, I'll be notorious. Or perhaps I'll lead the life of pleasure for a time and then – who knows? – rest and do nothing. What does Plato say is the highest end that man can attain here below? To sit down and contemplate the good. Perhaps that will be the end of me too. These things are on the knees of the gods. What will be, will be.

We were a little dazzled by his directness and surprised by the unexpected angle from which he looked at things. There was something foreign to us, and inconsequential, in his modes of thought, just as there was a suspicion of brogues in his pronunciation, and an unfamiliar turn in his phrasing. His qualities were not ordinary...And certainly Oscar Wilde was socially distinguished. It was impossible to overlook him in any company of College men.

WILLIAM WARD: *OSCAR WILDE: AN OXFORD REMINISCENCE*

Wilde was a personality from the first. His hair was much too long, sometimes parted in the middle, sometimes at the side, and he tossed it off his face with much the same gesture used by the flapper of today. His face was colourless, 'moonlike', with heavy eyes and thick lips; he had a perpetual simper and a convulsive laugh. He swayed as he walked, and lolled when at table. I never saw him run...His writing was huge and sprawling – somewhat like himself...Four words to a line was his normal allowance, and he took no notice of lines. One wonders if examiners ever mark by weight.

G. T. ATKINSON, 'OSCAR WILDE AT OXFORD', *THE CORNHILL MAGAZINE*, 1929

'A VERY AESTHETIC YOUNG MAN'

There is only one thing in the world worse than being talked about, and that is not being talked about.

THE PICTURE OF DORIAN GRAY

Beauty had existed long before 1880. It was Mr. Oscar Wilde who managed her debut…Fired by his fervid words, men and women hurled their mahogany into the streets and ransacked the curio-shops for furniture of Annish days. Dados arose upon every wall, sunflowers and the feathers of peacocks curved in every corner, tea grew quite cold while the guests were praising the Willow pattern of its cup.

MAX BEERBOHM, *1880*

There were few great houses in London where he was not known; fewer still where there was not among the younger generation an aggressive, irresponsible intolerance which had some relation, however vague, to his brilliant figure. Even athleticism rejoiced at this date to dissociate itself from anything that might have been in danger of easy approval from an older generation, by being too aesthetic; captains of university football teams had been seen with long hair.

R. H. GRETTON, *MODERN HISTORY OF THE ENGLISH PEOPLE*

A man who can dominate a London dinner-table can dominate the world. The future belongs to the dandy. It is the exquisites who are going to rule.

A WOMAN OF NO IMPORTANCE

I'm a very Sunflowery, Aprily showery,
Eastcheapy, Towery man.

I'm a very aesthetic young man,
A non energetic young man;

Slippity, sloppity over the shoppity,
Flippity flop young man.

I'm a bitter and mildly
Naturely childy,
Oscary Wildy man.

POPULAR SONG OF THE 1880S

If Mr Wilde were brought to this country with the view of illustrating in a public way his idea of the aesthetic...the general public would be interested in hearing from him a true and correct definition and explanation of this latest form of fashionable madness.

COL. W. F. MORSE, THE IMPRESARIO RICHARD D'OYLY CARTE'S
AMERICAN BUSINESS MANAGER, 8 NOVEMBER 1881

Of course, if one had enough money to go to America, one would not go.

Dear Colonel Morse, Will you kindly go to a good costumier (theatrical) for me and get them to make (you will not mention my name) two coats, to wear at matinées and perhaps in the evening. They should be beautiful, tight velvet doublet, with large flowered sleeves and little ruffs of cambric coming up from under collar...Any good costumier would know what I want – sort of Francis I dress: only knee-breeches instead of long hose...They were dreadfully disappointed at Cincinnati at my not wearing knee-breeches.

LETTER TO THE MANAGER OF WILDE'S AMERICAN TOUR

Oscar Wilde is here – an unclean beast.

HENRY JAMES

I have also lectured at Leadville, the great mining city in the Rocky Mountains...My audience was entirely miners; their make-up excellent, red shirts and blonde beards...I spoke to them of the early Florentines, and they slept as though no crime had ever

stained the ravines of their mountain home...Their sympathy touched me and I approached modern art and had almost won them over to a real reverence for what is beautiful when unluckily I described one of Jimmy Whistler's 'nocturnes in blue and gold'. Then they leaped to their feet and in their grand simple way swore that such things should not be.

LETTER TO MRS BERNARD BEERE

*M*ARRIAGE

LORD ILLINGWORTH: The Book of Life begins with a man and a
    woman in a garden.
MRS ALLONBY: It ends with Revelations.

A WOMAN OF NO IMPORTANCE

Her name is Constance, and she is quite young, very grave, and
mystical, with wonderful eyes, and dark brown coils of hair…We
are of course desperately in love. I have been obliged to be away
nearly all the time since our engagement, civilising the provinces
by my remarkable lectures, but we telegraph to each other twice a
day, and the telegraph clerks have become quite romantic in
consequence. I hand in my messages however very sternly, and try
to look as if 'love' was a cryptogram for 'buy Grand Trunks', and
'darling' a cypher for 'sell out at par.' I am sure it succeeds.

LETTER TO WALDO STORY

The one charm of marriage is that it makes a life of deception
absolutely necessary for both parties.

THE PICTURE OF DORIAN GRAY

Loveless marriages are horrible. But there is one thing worse than
an absolutely loveless marriage. A marriage in which there is love,
but on one side only; faith, but on one side only; devotion, but on
one side only and in which of the two hearts one is sure to be
broken.

AN IDEAL HUSBAND

I was delighted by his pretty wife and children, and his beautiful house designed by Godwin. He had a white dining room, the first I had seen, chairs, walls, cushions all white, but in the middle of the table a red cloth table-centre with a red terracotta statue and above it a red hanging lamp. I have never and shall never meet conversation that could match his...I was astonished by this scholar who as a man of the world was so perfect.

W. B. YEATS

*T*HE PICTURE OF DORIAN GRAY

There is no such thing as a moral or an immoral book. Books are well written, or badly written. That is all.

PREFACE TO *THE PICTURE OF DORIAN GRAY*

It was the strangest book that he had ever read. It seemed to him that in exquisite raiment, and to the delicate sound of flutes, the sins of the world were passing in dumb show before him. Things that he had dimly dreamed of were suddenly made real to him. Things of which he had never dreamed were gradually revealed.

It was a novel without a plot, and with only one character, being, indeed, simply a psychological study of a certain young Parisian, who spent his life trying to realise in the nineteenth century all the passions and modes of thought that belonged to every century except his own, and to sum up, as it were, in himself the various moods through which the world-spirit had ever passed, loving for their mere artificiality those renunciations that men have unwisely called virtue, as much as those natural rebellions that wise men still call sin. The style in which it was written was that curious jewelled style, vivid and obscure at once, full of argot and of archaisms, of technical expressions and of elaborate paraphrases, that characterises the work of some of the finest artists of the French school of *Symbolistes*. There were in it metaphors as monstrous as orchids, and as subtle in colour. The life of the senses was described in the terms of mystical philosophy. One hardly knew at times whether one was reading the spiritual ecstasies of some mediaeval saint or the morbid confessions of a modern sinner. It was a poisonous book.

THE PICTURE OF DORIAN GRAY

'IT IS PERSONALITIES, NOT PRINCIPLES,
THAT MOVE THE AGE'

Talk to every woman as if you loved her, and to every man as if he bored you, and at the end of your first season you will have the reputation of possessing the most perfect social tact.

A WOMAN OF NO IMPORTANCE

———

A fine intelligence and most wonderful talker.

MATTHEW ARNOLD

———

He was far and away the best talker I have ever met, with the most astounding gift of humour that irradiated all his other qualities...Whenever I meet anyone who knew Oscar Wilde at any period of his life, I am sure to hear a new story of him – some humorous or witty thing he had said...It was on the spur of the moment that Oscar's humour was so extraordinary, and it was this spontaneity that made him so wonderful a companion.

FRANK HARRIS

———

Wilde did not converse – he told tales. During the whole meal he hardly stopped. He spoke in a slow, musical tone, and his very voice was wonderful...Those who expected nothing from him got nothing, or only a little light froth, and as at first he used to give himself up to the task of amusing, many of those who thought they knew him will have known him only as the amuser.

ANDRÉ GIDE

———

That this talk was mostly a monologue was not his own fault. His manners were very good; he was careful to give his guests or his fellow-guests many a conversational opening, but seldom did anyone respond with more than a few words. Nobody was willing to interrupt the music of so magnificent a virtuoso. To have heard him consoled me for not having heard Dr Johnson or Edmund Burke, Lord Brougham or Sydney Smith.

MAX BEERBOHM

If one could only teach the English how to talk, and the Irish how to listen, society here would be quite civilised.

AN IDEAL HUSBAND

WILDE THE MAN

That face was almost an anachronism. It was like one of Holbein's portraits, a pale, large-featured individual: a peculiar, an interesting countenance of a singularly mild yet ardent expression…He wore his hair rather long, thrown back, and clustering about his neck like the hair of a medieval saint. He spoke with rapidity, in a low voice, with peculiarly distant enunciation; he spoke like a man who has made a study of expression. He listened like one accustomed to speak.

GEORGE FLEMING (JULIA CONSTANCE FLETCHER), *MIRAGE*, 1877 (A DESCRIPTION OF CLAUDE DAVENANT, A CHARACTER SUPPOSEDLY BASED ON OSCAR WILDE)

…[his face was] so colourless that a few pale freckles of good size were oddly conspicuous. He had a well-shaped mouth, with somewhat coarse lips and greenish hued teeth. The plainness of his face, however, was redeemed by the splendour of his great, eager eyes…He had one of the most alluring voices that I have ever listened to, round and soft, and full of variety and expression.

LILLIE LANGTRY, *THE DAYS I KNEW* (1925)

A big man, with a large pasty face, red cheeks, an ironic eye, bad and protrusive teeth, a vicious childlike mouth with lips soft with milk ready to suck some more. While he ate – and he ate little – he never stopped smoking opium-tainted Egyptian cigarettes.

MARCEL SCHWOB

…a great white caterpillar.

LADY COLIN CAMPBELL

18

26.

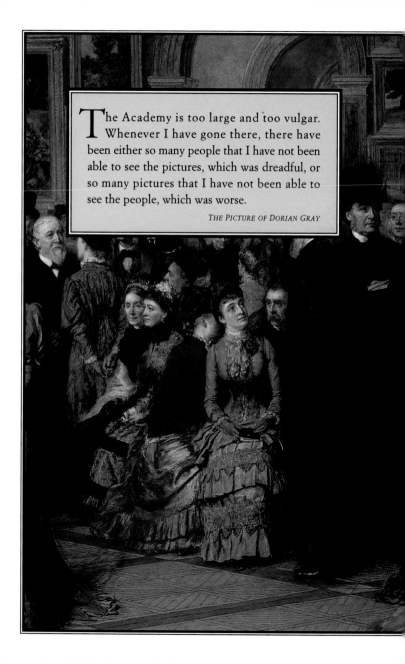

The Academy is too large and too vulgar. Whenever I have gone there, there have been either so many people that I have not been able to see the pictures, which was dreadful, or so many pictures that I have not been able to see the people, which was worse.

THE PICTURE OF DORIAN GRAY

$\mathcal{T}$HE CRITIC AS ARTIST

What is the difference between literature and journalism?
Oh! journalism is unreadable, and literature is not read. That is all.

THE CRITIC AS ARTIST

He who would stir us now by fiction must either give us an entirely new background, or reveal to us the soul of man in its innermost workings. The first is for the moment being done for us by Mr Rudyard Kipling. As one turns over the pages of his *Plain Tales from the Hills*, one feels as if one were seated under a palm-tree reading life by superb flashes of vulgarity. The bright colours of the bazaars dazzle one's eyes. The jaded, second-rate Anglo-Indians are in exquisite incongruity with their surroundings. The mere lack of style in the story-teller gives an odd journalistic realism to what he tells us. From the point of view of literature Mr Kipling is a genius who drops his aspirates. From the point of view of life, he is a reporter who knows vulgarity better than any one has ever known it. Dickens knew its clothes and its comedy. Mr Kipling knows its essence and its seriousness. He is our first authority on the second-rate, and has seen marvellous things through keyholes, and his backgrounds are real works of art. As for the second condition, we have had Browning, and Meredith is with us. But there is still much to be done in the sphere of intro-spection. People sometimes say that fiction is getting too morbid. As far as psychology is concerned, it has never been morbid enough. We have merely touched the surface of the soul, that is all. In one single ivory cell of the brain there are stored away things more marvellous and more terrible than even they have dreamed of, who, like the author of *Le Rouge et le Noir*, have

sought to track the soul into its most secret places, and to make life confess its dearest sins.

THE CRITIC AS ARTIST

What has Oscar in common with Art? except that he dines at our tables and picks from our platters the plums for the pudding he peddles in the provinces... Oscar – the amiable, irresponsible, esurient Oscar – with no more sense of a picture than of the fit of a coat, has the courage of the opinions of others!

JAMES MCNEILL WHISTLER, *THE WORLD*, 17 NOVEMBER 1886

*L*ADY WINDERMERE'S FAN

I took the drama, the most objective form known to art, and made it as personal a mode of expression as the lyric or the sonnet, at the same time that I widened its range and enriched its characterisation: drama, novel, poem in rhyme, poem in prose, subtle or fantastic dialogue, whatever I touched I made beautiful in a new mode of beauty: to truth itself I gave what is false no less than what is true as its rightful province, and showed that the false and the true are merely forms of intellectual existence. I treated Art as the supreme reality, and life as a mere mode of fiction.

DE PROFUNDIS

The man or woman who does not chuckle with delight at the good things which abound in *Lady Windermere's Fan* should consult a physician at once.

A. B. WALKLEY

CECIL GRAHAM: What is a cynic? *(Sitting on the back of the sofa)*

LORD DARLINGTON: A man who knows the price of everything and the value of nothing.

CECIL GRAHAM: And a sentimentalist, my dear Darlington, is a man who sees an absurd value in everything, and doesn't know the market price of any single thing.

LORD DARLINGTON: You always amuse me, Cecil. You talk as if you were a man of experience.

CECIL GRAHAM: I am. *(Moves up to front of fireplace)*

LORD DARLINGTON: You are far too young!

CECIL GRAHAM: That is a great error. Experience is a question of instinct about life. I have got it. Tuppy hasn't. Experience is the name Tuppy gives to his mistakes. That is all.

LADY WINDERMERE'S FAN

Black satin

Velvet lined unke

BEATON

Mrs Erlynne   Act III   Lady Windermere's Fan.

*A*N IDEAL HUSBAND

When we go to see a piece by Mr Oscar Wilde we find ourselves at once among the aristocracy. In *An Ideal Husband*, for example, anyone who is anybody has a title, or is related to one…The fact is, that Mr Oscar Wilde is a very superior person, and must have around him superior people and things.

THE ILLUSTRATED SPORTING AND DRAMATIC NEWS

LORD GORING:…Fashion is what one wears oneself. What is unfashionable is what other people wear.

PHIPPS: Yes, my lord.

LORD GORING: Just as vulgarity is simply the conduct of other people.

PHIPPS: Yes, my lord.

LORD GORING: Other people are quite dreadful. The only possible society is oneself.

PHIPPS: Yes, my lord.

LORD GORING: To love oneself is the beginning of a lifelong romance, Phipps.

PHIPPS: Yes, my lord.

AN IDEAL HUSBAND

In a certain sense Mr Wilde is to me our only thorough playwright. He plays with everything: with wit, with philosophy, with drama, with actors and audiences, with the whole theatre.

GEORGE BERNARD SHAW ON *AN IDEAL HUSBAND*

B.326 B.325

B.327.
PINK

*T*HE VELVET UNDERGROUND

THE YOUNG SYRIAN: She is very beautiful tonight.

FIRST SOLDIER: The Tetrarch has a sombre look.

SECOND SOLDIER: Yes, he has a sombre look.

FIRST SOLDIER: He is looking at something.

SECOND SOLDIER: He is looking at some one.

FIRST SOLDIER: At whom is he looking?

SECOND SOLDIER: I cannot tell.

THE YOUNG SYRIAN: How pale the Princess is! Never have I seen her so pale. She is like the shadow of a white rose in a mirror of silver.

THE PAGE OF HERODIAS: You must not look at her. You look too much at her.

FIRST SOLDIER: Herodias has filled the cup of the Tetrarch.

THE CAPPADOCIAN: Is that the Queen Herodias, she who wears a black mitre sewn with pearls, and whose hair is powdered with blue dust?

FIRST SOLDIER: Yes, that is Herodias, the Tetrarch's wife.

SALOME

SALOME: Give me the head of Jokanaan.

HEROD: ...I have topazes, yellow as are the eyes of tigers, and topazes that are pink as the eyes of a wood-pigeon, and green topazes that are as the eyes of cats. I have opals that burn always with an ice-like flame, opals that make sad men's minds, and are fearful of the shadows. I have onyxes like the eyeballs of a dead woman. I have moonstones that change when the moon changes, and are wan when they see the sun. I have sapphires big like eggs and as blue as blue flowers. The sea wanders within them and the moon comes never to trouble the blue of their waves. I have chrysolites and beryls and chrysoprases and rubies. I have sardonyx and hyacinth stones, and stones of chalcedony, and I will give them all to you, all, and other things will I add to them. The King of the Indies has but even now sent me four fans fashioned from the feathers of parrots, and the King of Numidia a garment of ostrich feathers. I have a crystal, into which it is not lawful for a woman to look, nor may young men behold it until they have been beaten with rods. In a coffer of nacre I have three wondrous turquoises. He who wears them on his forehead can imagine things which are not, and he who carries them in his hand can make women sterile. These are great treasures above all price. They are treasures without price. But this is not all. In an ebony coffer I have two cups of amber, that are like apples of gold. If an enemy pour poison into these cups, they become like an apple of silver. In a coffer incrusted with amber I have sandals incrusted with glass. I have mantles that have been brought from the land of the Seres, and bracelets decked about with carbuncles and with jade that come from the city of Euphrates...What desirest thou more than this, Salomé?

Tell me the thing that thou desirest, and I will give it thee. All that thou askest I will give thee save one thing. I will give thee all that is mine, save one life. I will give thee the mantle of the high priest. I will give thee the veil of the sanctuary.

THE JEWS: Oh! Oh!

SALOME: Give me the head of Jokanaan.

HEROD: Let her be given what she asks! Of a truth she is her mother's child!

SALOME

31

JACK: I have a country house with some land, of course, attached to it, about fifteen hundred acres, I believe; but I don't depend on that for my real income. In fact, as far as I can make out, the poachers are the only people who make anything out of it.

LADY BRACKNELL: A country house! How many bedrooms? Well, that point can be cleared up afterwards. You have a town house, I hope? A girl with a simple, unspoiled nature, like Gwendolen, could hardly be expected to reside in the country.

JACK: Well, I own a house in Belgrave Square, but it is let by the year to Lady Bloxham. Of course, I can get it back whenever I like, at six months' notice.

LADY BRACKNELL: Lady Bloxham? I don't know her.

JACK: Oh, she goes about very little. She is a lady considerably advanced in years.

LADY BRACKNELL: Ah, nowadays that is no guarantee of respectability of character. What number in Belgrave Square?

JACK: 149.

LADY BRACKNELL (*shaking her head*): The unfashionable side. I thought there was something. However, that could easily be altered.

JACK: Do you mean the fashion, or the side?

LADY BRACKNELL (*sternly*): Both, if necessary, I presume. What are your politics?

JACK: Well, I am afraid I really have none. I am a Liberal Unionist.

LADY BRACKNELL: Oh, they count as Tories. They dine with us. Or come in the evening at any rate. You have, of course, no sympathy of any kind with the Radical Party?

JACK: Oh! I don't want to put the asses against the classes, if that is what you mean, Lady Bracknell.

LADY BRACKNELL: That is exactly what I do mean...ahem! ...Are your parents living?

JACK: I have lost both my parents.

LADY BRACKNELL: Both?...To lose one parent may be regarded as a misfortune...to lose both seems like carelessness. Who was your father? He was evidently a man of some wealth. Was he born in what the Radical papers call the purple of commerce, or did he rise from the ranks of the aristocracy?

JACK: I am afraid I really don't know. The fact is, Lady Bracknell, I said I had lost my parents. It would be nearer the truth to say that my parents seemed to have lost me...I don't actually know who I am by birth. I was...well, I was found.

LADY BRACKNELL: Found!

JACK: The late Mr Thomas Cardew, an old gentleman of a very charitable and kindly disposition, found me, and gave me the name of Worthing, because he happened to have a first-class ticket for Worthing in his pocket at the time. Worthing is a place in Sussex. It is a seaside resort.

LADY BRACKNELL: Where did the charitable gentleman who had a first-class ticket for this seaside resort find you?

JACK (*gravely*): In a hand-bag.

LADY BRACKNELL: A hand-bag?

JACK (*very seriously*): Yes, Lady Bracknell. I was in a hand-bag – a somewhat large, black leather hand-bag, with handles to it – an ordinary hand-bag in fact.

LADY BRACKNELL: In what locality did this Mr James, or Thomas, Cardew come across this ordinary hand-bag?

JACK: In the cloak-room at Victoria Station. It was given to him in mistake for his own.

LADY BRACKNELL: The cloak-room at Victoria Station?

JACK: Yes. The Brighton line.

LADY BRACKNELL: The line is immaterial. Mr Worthing, I confess I feel somewhat bewildered by what you have just told me. To be born, or at any rate bred, in a hand-bag, whether it had handles or not, seems to me to display a contempt for the ordinary decencies of family life that reminds one of the worst excesses of the French Revolution. And I presume you know what that unfortunate movement led to? As for the particular locality in which the hand-bag was found, a cloak-room at a railway station might serve to conceal a social indiscretion – has probably, indeed, been used for that purpose before now – but it could hardly be regarded as an assured basis for a recognised position in good society.

THE IMPORTANCE OF BEING EARNEST

The real charm of the play, if it is to have a charm, must be in the
dialogue. The plot is slight, but, I think, adequate…Well, I think
an amusing thing with lots of wit and fun might be made.

LETTER TO GEORGE ALEXANDER

It is, we were told last night, 'much harder to listen to nonsense
than to talk it', but not if it is good nonsense. And very good
nonsense, excellent fooling, in this new play of Mr Oscar Wilde's.
It is, indeed, as new a new comedy as we have had this year.

PALL MALL GAZETTE, 15 FEBRUARY 1895

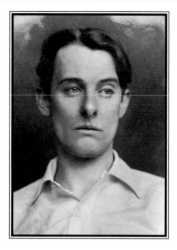

My Own Boy, Your sonnet is quite lovely, and it is a marvel that those red rose-leaf lips of yours should have been made no less for music of song than for madness of kisses. Your slim gilt soul walks between passion and poetry. I know Hyacinthus, whom Apollo loved so madly, was you in Greek days.

Why are you alone in London, and when do you go to Salisbury? Do go there to cool your hands in the grey twilight of Gothic things, and come here whenever you like. It is a lovely place – it only lacks you; but go to Salisbury first. Always, with undying love,

Yours,

OSCAR

Letter to Lord Alfred Douglas, the 22-year-old son of the 8th Marquess of Queensberry, January 1893 – subsequently used in attempted blackmail, finally read out in court during Wilde's trials

I will begin by telling you that I blame myself terribly. As I sit here in this dark cell in convict clothes, a disgraced and ruined man, I blame myself. In the perturbed and fitful nights of anguish, in the long monotonous days of pain, it is myself I blame. I blame myself for allowing an unintellectual friendship, a friendship whose primary aim was not the creation and contemplation of beautiful things, to entirely dominate my life. From the very first there was too wide a gap between us…While you were with me you were the absolute ruin of my Art, and in allowing you to stand persistently between Art and myself I give to myself shame and blame in the fullest degree.

DE PROFUNDIS

Supplement to the 'New Rattle' — May 20th 1873.

A dream of Decadence on the Cherwell.
by our Decayed Artist.

THE SPHINX

Your lovers are not dead, I know. They will rise
    up and hear your voice
And clash their cymbals and rejoice and run to
    kiss your mouth! And so,

Set wings upon your argosies! Set horses to your
    ebon car!
Back to your Nile! Or if you are grown sick of
    dead divinities

Follow some roving lion's spoor across the copper-
    coloured plain,
Reach out and hale him by the mane and bid him
    be your paramour!

Couch by his side upon the grass and set your white
    teeth in his throat
And when you hear his dying note lash your long
    flanks of polished brass

And take a tiger for your mate, whose amber sides
    are flecked with black,
And ride upon his gilded back in triumph through
    the Theban gate,

And toy with him in amorous jests, and when he
    turns, and snarls, and gnaws,
O smite him with your jasper claws! and bruise
    him with your agate breasts!

THE SPHINX

ℱEASTING WITH PANTHERS

Tired of being on the heights I deliberately went to the depths in the search for new sensations. What the paradox was to me in the sphere of thought, perversity became to me in the sphere of passion. Desire, at the end, was a malady, or a madness, or both.

DE PROFUNDIS

We caught the tread of dancing feet,
We loitered down the moonlit street,
And stopped beneath the harlot's house.

Inside, above the din and fray,
We heard the loud musicians play
The 'Treues Liebes Herz' of Strauss.

Like strange mechanical grotesques,
Making fantastic arabesques,
The shadows raced across the blind.

We watched the ghostly dancers spin
To sound of horn and violin,
Like black leaves wheeling in the wind.

Like wire-pulled automatons,
Slim silhouetted skeletons
Went sidling through the slow quadrille.

They took each other by the hand,
And danced a stately saraband;
Their laughter echoed thin and shrill.

THE HARLOT'S HOUSE

People thought it dreadful of me to have entertained at dinner the evil things of life, and to have found pleasure in their company. But they, from the point of view through which I, as an artist in life, approached them, were delightfully suggestive and stimulating. It was like feasting with panthers. The danger was half the excitement. I used to feel as the snake-charmer must feel when he lures the cobra to stir from the painted cloth or reed-basket that holds it, and makes it spread its hood at his bidding, and sway to and fro in the air as a plant sways restfully in a stream. They were to me the brightest of gilded snakes. Their poison was part of their perfection.

DE PROFUNDIS

*T*HE SOUL OF AN INDIVIDUAL

There are three kinds of despots. There is the despot who tyrannises over the body. There is the despot who tyrannises over the soul. There is the despot who tyrannises over the soul and body alike. The first is called the Prince. The second is called the Pope. The third is called the People. The Prince may be cultivated. Many princes have been. Yet in the Prince there is danger...The Pope may be cultivated. Many Popes have been...Yet...it is better for the artist not to live with Popes...It is impossible for the artist to live with the People. All despots bribe. The People bribe and brutalise. Who told them to exercise authority?...Who taught them the trick of tyranny?

...The past is what man should not have been. The present is what man ought not to be. The future is what artists are.

It will, of course, be said that such a scheme as is set forth here is quite unpractical, and goes against human nature. This is perfectly true. It is unpractical, and it goes against human nature. This is why it is worth carrying out, and that is why one proposes it. For what is a practical scheme? A practical scheme is either a scheme that is already in existence, or a scheme that could be carried out under existing conditions. But it is exactly the existing conditions that one objects to; and any scheme that could accept these conditions is wrong and foolish. The conditions will be done away with, and human nature will change...

Individualism will also be unselfish and unaffected. It has been pointed out that one of the results of the extraordinary tyranny of authority is that words are absolutely distorted from their proper and simple meaning, and are used to express the observe of their right signification. What is true about Art is true about Life. A man is called affected, nowadays, if he dresses as he likes to dress.

But in doing that he is acting in a perfectly natural manner. Affectation, in such matters, consists in dressing, according to the views of one's neighbour, whose views, as they are the views of the majority, will probably be extremely stupid. Or a man is called selfish if he lives in the manner that seems to him most suitable for the full realisation of his own personality; if, in fact, the primary aim of his life is self-development. But this is the way in which every one should live. Selfishness is not living as one wishes to live, it is asking others to live as one wishes to live. And unselfishness is letting other people's lives alone, not interfering with them. Selfishness always aims at creating around it an absolute uniformity of type. Unselfishness recognises infinite variety of type as a delightful thing, accepts it, acquiesces in it, enjoys it. It is not selfish to think for oneself. A man who does not think for himself does not think at all. It is grossly selfish to require of one's neighbour that he should think in the same way, and hold the same opinions. Why should he? If he can think, he will probably think differently. If he cannot think, it is monstrous to require thought of any kind from him...

What man has sought for is, indeed, neither pain nor pleasure, but simply Life. Man has sought to live intensely, fully, perfectly. When he can do so without exercising restraint on others, or suffering it ever, and his activities are all pleasurable to him, he will be saner, healthier, more civilised, more himself. Pleasure is Nature's test, her sign of approval. When man is happy, he is in harmony with himself and his environment.

THE SOUL OF MAN UNDER SOCIALISM

THE WIT OF WILDE

One should never trust a woman who tells one her real age. A woman who would tell one that, would tell one anything.

If a woman wants to hold a man, she has merely to appeal to the worst in him.

All women become like their mothers. That is their tragedy. No man does. That is his.

Sentiment is all very well for the buttonhole. But the essential thing for a necktie is style. A well-tied tie is the first serious step in life.

Children begin by loving their parents; after a time they judge them. Rarely, if ever, do they forgive them.

There is nothing like youth. The middle-aged are mortgaged to Life. The old are in life's lumber-room. But youth is the Lord of Life. Youth has a kingdom waiting for it.

The youth of the present day are quite monstrous. They have absolutely no respect for dyed hair.

It is absurd to divide people into good and bad. People are either charming or tedious.

The English country gentleman galloping after a fox – the unspeakable in full pursuit of the uneatable.

I adore simple pleasures. They are the last refuge of the complex.

A cigarette is the perfect type of a perfect pleasure. It is exquisite, and it leaves one unsatisfied. What more can one want?

Anybody can write a three-volume novel. It merely requires a complete ignorance of both life and literature.

The only way to get rid of a temptation is to yield to it.

Indiscretion is the better part of valour.

Anything becomes a pleasure if one does it too often.

Punctuality is the thief of time.

When a man says that he has exhausted Life, one knows that life has exhausted him.

THE SCARLET MARQUESS

A man cannot be too careful in his choice of enemies.

THE PICTURE OF DORIAN GRAY

Your intimacy with this man Wilde…It must either cease or I will disown you and stop all money supplies. I am not going to try and analyse this intimacy, and I make no charge; but to my mind to pose as a thing is as bad as to be it…

Your disgusted, so-called father, QUEENSBERRY.

MARQUESS OF QUEENSBERRY TO LORD ALFRED DOUGLAS, 1 APRIL 1894

WHAT A FUNNY LITTLE MAN YOU ARE

TELEGRAM FROM LORD ALFRED DOUGLAS TO HIS FATHER, 2 APRIL 1894

Dearest Bobbie, Since I saw you something has happened. Bosie's father has left a card at my club with hideous words on it. I don't see anything now but a criminal prosecution. My whole life seems ruined by this man. The tower of ivory is assailed by the foul thing. On the sand is my life spilt. I don't know what to do.

OSCAR WILDE TO ROBERT ROSS, 28 FEBRUARY 1895

The one disgraceful, unpardonable, and to all time contemptible action of my life was my allowing myself to be forced into appealing to Society for help and protection against your father…Of course once I had put into motion the forces of Society, Society turned on me and said, 'Have you been living all this time in defiance of my

laws, and do you now appeal to those laws for protection? You shall have those laws exercised to the full. You shall abide by what you have appealed to.'

DE PROFUNDIS

There is not a man or woman in the English-speaking world possessed of the treasure of a wholesome mind who is not under a deep debt of gratitude to the Marquess of Queensberry for destroying the High Priest of the Decadents. The obscene imposter, whose prominence has been a social outrage ever since he transferred from Trinity Dublin to Oxford his vices, his follies, and his vanities, has been exposed, and that thoroughly at last. But to the exposure there must be legal and social sequels. There must be another trial at the Old Bailey, or a coroner's inquest – the latter for choice; and of the Decadents, of their hideous conceptions of the meaning of Art, of their worse than Eleusinian mysteries, there must be an absolute end.

THE NATIONAL OBSERVER

THE LOVE THAT DARE NOT
SPEAK ITS NAME

THE ARREST OF OSCAR WILDE

What is the 'Love that dare not speak its name'?

The 'Love that dare not speak its name' in this century is such a great affection of an elder for a younger man as there was between David and Jonathan, such as Plato made the very basis of his philosophy, and such as you find in the sonnets of

Michaelangelo and Shakespeare. It is that deep, spiritual affection that is as pure as it is perfect. It dictates and pervades great works of art like those of Shakespeare and Michaelangelo, and those two letters of mine, such as they are. It is in this century misunderstood, so much misunderstood that it may be described as the 'Love that dare not speak its name', and on account of it I am placed where I am now. It is beautiful, it is fine, it is the noblest form of affection. There is nothing unnatural about it. It is intellectual, and it repeatedly exists between an elder and a younger man, when the elder man has intellect, and the younger man has all the joy, hope and glamour of life before him. That it should be so the world does not understand. The world mocks at it and sometimes puts one in the pillory for it.

OSCAR WILDE, AT HIS FIRST TRIAL, 26 APRIL 1895

It is no use for me to address you. People who can do these things must be dead to all sense of shame, and one cannot hope to produce any effect upon them. It is the worst case I have ever tried...that you, Wilde, have been the centre of a circle of extensive corruption of the most hideous kind among young men, it is equally impossible to doubt...I shall, under such circumstances, be expected to pass the severest sentence that the law allows. In my judgement it is totally inadequate for such a case as this. The sentence of the Court is that each of you be imprisoned and kept to hard labour for two years.

MR JUSTICE WILLS, PRONOUNCING SENTENCE AFTER THE SECOND TRIAL, 25 MAY 1895

The remarkable part of the interview was that Oscar hardly talked at all except to ask if there were any chance of his being let out, what the attitude of the press and public would be, as to whether any of the present Government would be favourably disposed towards him. He cried the whole time and when we asked *him* to talk more he said he had nothing to say and wanted to hear *us* talk. That as you know is very unlike Oscar...I firmly and honestly believe apart from all prejudice that he is simply wasting and pining away, to use the old cliché he is sinking under a broken heart...If asked whether he was going to die, it seems quite possible within the next few months, even if his constitution remained unimpaired, but for the causes that wives and husbands die shortly after each other, for no particular cause.

ROBERT ROSS, LETTER TO MORE ADEY, 1896

People nowadays do not understand what cruelty is. They regard it as a sort of terrible mediaeval passion...(but) ordinary cruelty is simply stupidity. It is the entire want of imagination. It is the result in our days of stereotyped systems, of hard-and-fast rules, and of stupidity. Wherever there is centralisation there is stupidity. What is inhuman in modern life is officialism. Authority is as destructive to those who exercise it as it is to those on whom it is exercised. It is the Prison Board, and the system that it carries out, that is the primary source of the cruelty that is exercised on a child in prison. The people who uphold the system have excellent intentions. Those who carry it out are humane in intention also. Responsibility is shifted on to the disciplinary regulations. It is supposed that because a thing is the rule it is right.

The present treatment of children is terrible, primarily from

people not understanding the peculiar psychology of a child's nature. A child can understand a punishment inflicted by an individual, such as a parent or guardian, and bear it with a certain amount of acquiescence. What it cannot understand is a punishment inflicted by society. It cannot realise what society is. With grown people it is, of course, the reverse. Those of us who are either in prison or have been sent there, can understand, and do understand, what that collective force called society means, and whatever we may think of its methods or claims, we can force ourselves to accept it. Punishment inflicted on us by an individual, on the other hand, is a thing that no grown person endures, or is expected to endure.

...The terror of a child in prison is quite limitless...Every child is confined to its cell for twenty-three hours out of the twenty-four. This is the appalling thing. To shut up a child in a dimly lit cell, for twenty-three hours out of the twenty-four, is an example of the cruelty of stupidity. If an individual, parent or guardian, did this to a child, he would be severely punished...But inhuman treatment by society is to the child the more terrible because there is no appeal.

LETTER TO THE EDITOR OF *THE DAILY CHRONICLE*, 28 MAY 1897

With slouch and swing around the ring
   We trod the Fools' Parade!
We did not care: we knew we were
   The Devil's Own Brigade:
And shaven head and feet of lead
   Make a merry masquerade.

We tore the tarry rope to shreds
   With blunt and bleeding nails;
We rubbed the doors, and scrubbed the floors,
   And cleaned the shining rails;
And, rank by rank, we soaped the plank,
   And clattered with the pails.

We sewed the sacks, we broke the stones,
   We turned the dusty drill:
We banged the tins, and bawled the hymns,
   And sweated on the mill:
But in the heart of every man
   Terror was lying still.

So still it lay that every day
   Crawled like a weed-clogged wave:
And we forgot the bitter lot

That waits for fool and knave,
Till once, as we tramped in from work,
  We passed an open grave.

With yawning mouth the yellow hole
  Gaped for a living thing;
The very mud cried out for blood
  To the thirsty asphalte ring:
And we knew that ere one dawn grew fair
  Some prisoner had to swing.

Right in we went, with soul intent
  On Death and Dread and Doom:
The hangman, with his little bag,
  Went shuffling through the gloom:
And I trembled as I groped my way
  Into my numbered tomb.

———◆———

And all men kill the thing they love,
  By all let this be heard,
Some do it with a bitter look,
  Some with a flattering word,
The coward does it with a kiss,
  The brave man with a sword!

THE BALLAD OF READING GAOL

Everything about my tragedy has been hideous, mean, repellent, lacking in style. Our very dress makes us grotesques. We are the zanies of sorrow. We are clowns whose hearts are broken.

DE PROFUNDIS

An Eternity of Infamy

I have come, not from obscurity into the momentary notoriety of crime, but from a sort of eternity of fame to a sort of eternity of infamy.

De Profundis

OBITUARY

A Reuter telegram from Paris states that Oscar Wilde died there yesterday afternoon from meningitis. The melancholy end to a career which once promised so well is stated to have come in an obscure hotel of the Latin Quarter. Here the once brilliant man of letters was living, exiled from his country and from the society of his countrymen. The verdict that a jury passed upon his conduct at the Old Bailey in May, 1895, destroyed for ever his reputation, and condemned him to ignoble obscurity for the remainder of his days. When he had served his sentence of two years' imprisonment, he was broken in health as well as bankrupt in fame and fortune. Death has soon ended what must have been a life of wretchedness and unavailing regret.

THE TIMES, 1 DECEMBER 1900

Though his death has been a great shock to those who knew him as well as I did, it was in many ways for the best. He was very unhappy, and would have become more unhappy as time went on. In most cases this is said merely as a matter of form and a convention of comfort but in this particular instance it really *can* be said with perfect truth.

ROBERT ROSS, LETTER TO LOUIS WILKINSON, 10 DECEMBER 1900

And alien tears will fill for him
    Pity's long-broken urn,
For his mourners will be outcast men,
    And outcasts always mourn.

I heard his golden voice and marked him trace
Under the common thing the hidden grace,
And conjure wonder out of emptiness,
Till mean things put on beauty like a dress
And all the world was an enchanted place.

LORD ALFRED DOUGLAS, *THE DEAD POET*

PICTURE CREDITS

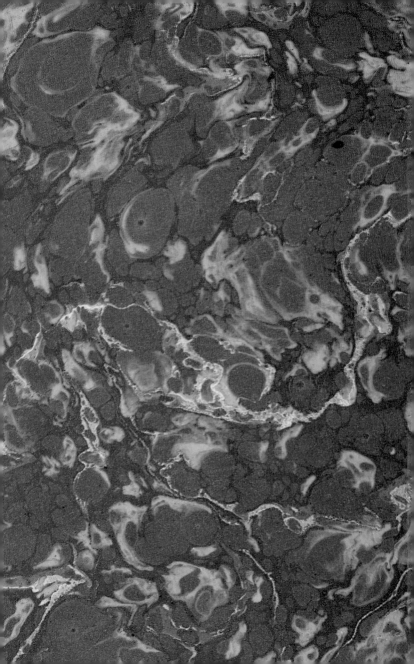